FRANKLIN THE FEARLESS
AND HIS GREATEST TREASURE

A Thomas and Matthew Adventure

ISBN 978-1-64670-747-8 (Paperback)
ISBN 978-1-64670-748-5 (Hardcover)
ISBN 978-1-64670-749-2 (Digital)

Covenant Books, Inc.
11661 Hwy 707
Murrells Inlet, SC 29576
www.covenantbooks.com

FRANKLIN THE FEARLESS
AND HIS GREATEST TREASURE

A Thomas and Matthew Adventure

Patrick Pickett

There were two young brothers named Thomas and Matthew. They lived in a neighborhood with a nearby park where they loved to play and explore. Thomas and Matthew were adventurous boys who loved having their daddy read to them. It helped them to imagine having adventures in far-off lands.

One evening before bed, Thomas and Matthew asked Daddy to read them a pirate story, one about life on the seven seas looking for treasure.

Daddy said, "I have just the story for you boys. This story is about Franklin the Fearless, the most fearless pirate in all the seven seas. Because the word *fear* was in his name, everyone feared him and no one wanted to be his friend."

"Standing in front of his ship one day, Franklin the Fearless had an idea. He shouted out to everyone that if they would be his friend, he would tell them about his greatest treasure. As everyone gathered around, he told the tale of how he found his greatest treasure ever."

At that point, Thomas and Matthew drifted off to sleep.

When they woke up the next day, Thomas said to Matthew, "Why don't we become pirates and find Franklin the Fearless' treasure? I can be Thomas the Terrible, and you can be Matthew the Mean."

Matthew replied, "What a great idea! Let's find the treasure so we can show Daddy that we are real pirates."

The boys went to the basketball court first because the lines there resembled lines on a treasure map.

They explored all around. Thomas and Matthew looked at every line and their imaginations ran wild. What did the lines mean? Did they point to a direction? Surely there had to be a clue somewhere.

Next, the boys went to the sunken ground behind their home that looked like the entrance to a secret cave.

Thomas and Matthew looked everywhere for some treasure. They looked behind bushes and under rocks. They explored the entire area and could not find any signs of pirates or treasure.

Then Thomas and Matthew went to the pond that reminded them of a lagoon. Pirates always buried treasure by a lagoon. The boys looked for pirate footprints near the water. They looked for an 'X marks the spot' and dig marks.

The boys looked and looked 'til finally Thomas said to Matthew, "There HAS to be treasure around here somewhere!"

Lastly, the boys went to the swimming pool to see if they could see a pirate ship. The blue water looked like the open ocean, but there was no ship or treasure in sight.

The boys went back home feeling defeated. They told Daddy all the places they had looked to find Franklin the Fearless' greatest treasure.

Daddy said, "Why don't we go look together at all the places you looked? We'll see if we can find any clues to Franklin the Fearless' treasure. When we come back, we can finish reading the story."

Thomas the Terrible and Matthew the Mean began to feel hopeful.

Daddy told the boys, "Let's go to the basketball court that looks like a treasure map and see if there is a clue."

Thomas and Matthew nodded in agreement.

As they approached, Daddy asked the boys, "What do you see?"

"Nothing, Daddy," replied Thomas in a disappointed tone.

"I see a clue," said Daddy.

"Where?" Matthew asked.

"See those baby kittens in the grass by the fence? They are scared. Let's watch for a minute and see what happens."

A moment later, a momma cat appeared to comfort her scared little kittens. She let out a gentle meow and led the kittens home to safety.

Daddy told the boys, "Mommas come in all different shapes and sizes. Sometimes they are people, but they can be animals too. The clue to our greatest treasure is that mommas are always listening to us. When we are scared, mommas are the first to come to our side and comfort us."

"Let's go to the sunken ground and see what clues we find there."

When they got to the sunken ground, they heard a loud chirping sound from a bird in a tree.

Daddy pointed up and said, "Matthew and Thomas, do you see the nest? A baby bird must have fallen out of the tree, and the momma is trying to find her baby. Let's look around."

Matthew pointed at the ground and exclaimed, "I found it!"

Daddy gently picked up the fragile baby bird and placed it in the nest next to the momma. The momma bird looked at Daddy as if to say thank you and began feeding her baby.

Daddy said, "Mommas are so good at working hard that many times we don't notice when they might need help. It's up to us to pay attention and find out when Momma needs our help. Okay, boys, on to the pond to see if we can find another clue."

When Daddy and the boys reached the pond, they noticed a momma duck waiting patiently across the street from the pond. Drivers got out of their cars and helped stop traffic so that the momma duck and her ducklings could safely cross to cool off in the water. Once the ducks were across, the drivers got back into their cars and went on their way.

"Boys, another clue is how the momma duck taught her ducklings to be patient so that they could make a good choice about when to cross the road safely," said Daddy.

"Last but not least, let's go look by the pool. Why don't we stop at home first and grab our swimsuits and towels? Then we can cool off after our long afternoon of treasure hunting."

As Daddy unlocked the pool gate, he reminded the boys, "This is locked to keep young kids from swimming alone, so they will stay safe."

After Daddy and the boys swam for a while, a young mother and her child got into the water.

Thomas whispered to Daddy, "Look Daddy, there's a momma with her baby!"

Daddy greeted the young mother and smiled. Then he said, "Well boys, it's time to go home and change. Then we can finish our pirate story."

Back at home, Daddy picked up the book about Franklin the Fearless and continued to read.

*****

Franklin began to spin his tale about his greatest treasure. The other pirates listened as he talked about all the places he had been and the adventures he had had in his life.

"You see, daddies teach us about building things, having adventures, and the value of hard work. My daddy taught me how to become a good pirate, to have respect for others, and to never give up."

Franklin continued, "My momma's name is Wanda the Watchful. She gave me the name Franklin the Fearless because I was always the first one in our family to try something new. Sometimes trying something new meant that I got hurt, and Momma was always there to help me get through it.

"When I got my own pirate ship, I named it after Momma. It has always steered me in the right direction and helped me find my way home. Momma taught me about patience, virtue, and honesty and that the greatest reward for hard work isn't a pat on the back. It is knowing that you did your best.

"Mommas give us encouragement and strength, and they are always rooting for us to be successful. I believe that mommas are a window to heaven because mommas give their whole lives to their family, and there is no greater love than that. This is why my greatest treasure is my momma."

"The end…or is it?" asked Daddy as he closed the book. He continued, "Franklin the Fearless was right. No one works harder than Momma. She quietly works in the background making our house run like a fine machine, and she often doesn't stop until everyone else has been taken care of. Mommas are the best listeners. They know when we are sad or hurt, and they know just what to do or say to make us feel better. Boys, do you know what *our* greatest treasure is?"

"Yes!" they shouted in unison.

"Great!" said Daddy, "I will be right back."

The boys watched with big eyes as Daddy returned with an old-looking chest.

"Thomas and Matthew, because you know now what real treasure is, we're going to fill this chest with things for Momma that she will love. Things like pictures, mementos, and notes to Momma from us. We can add special things whenever she has a birthday, on Mother's Day, or at Christmas."

"Why don't we choose something special today to put in here for Momma. There is a special day coming up soon, and we can surprise her! She will be really happy."

Thomas went and wrote a note to Momma, telling her how much he loved her, and Matthew went and found his favorite toy car because he could not write yet. Daddy added his favorite wedding picture because he wanted Momma to know how beautiful she was to him.

"Now when Momma comes home, we can talk about our treasure hunt but not about our surprise. Okay, boys?"

Matthew and Thomas agreed, and Daddy quietly put the box back in its hiding spot.

Daddy hid the box just in time because the door opened, and Momma came in with an armload of groceries. When the groceries were put away, Momma sat down with Thomas and Matthew. She listened carefully while they told her about their adventure.

Thomas told Momma how he was Thomas the Terrible and Matthew was Matthew the Mean and that they had been pirates looking for treasure while Momma was out. They told her about all the places they had searched and what they had seen.

Momma replied, "That sounds like a lot of fun! But I don't think you are terrible, Thomas. And I don't think that Matthew is mean. Thomas, you are Thomas the Terrific, and Matthew is Matthew the Magnificent. You both are very good boys, and you are the kind of boys any mom and dad could be proud of!"

It was getting late, so Momma and Daddy tucked the boys in to their beds, and they had wonderful dreams about their adventure.

The next day, Daddy told Thomas and Matthew that the special day had arrived. It was Momma and Daddy's wedding anniversary and time to give Momma their surprise. Matthew and Thomas were so excited, they could hardly wait.

Daddy went to the hiding spot and brought out the special chest. He said, "Happy Anniversary, Beautiful! This is for you from the boys and I." Daddy always used endearments for Momma like "Gorgeous," "Beautiful," or "Doll."

The chest had an old-looking lock with a skeleton key. As Daddy put the box beside Momma and gave her the key, Momma exclaimed, "What could this be?"

Daddy said, "Open it, Doll," as the boys giggled with excitement.

Momma put the key in the lock and twisted carefully until it opened. Then she gently lifted the lid, and a big smile spread across her face.

Momma lifted the wedding picture and the note from Daddy saying it was his favorite picture. He wrote that he was very thankful Momma had chosen to build their family with him.

Next, Momma lifted out the letter from Thomas that thanked her for all the times she had fixed things when he was sad or hurt. He told her he was happy that she knew what his favorite food was.

Matthew watched as Momma took out his favorite car. He gave her a great big Matthew hug and said, "Momma, you have bought me lots of toy cars, but you don't have one of your own. I am giving you one so that you can play with me and Thomas."

At the very bottom of the chest was an anniversary card. Momma lifted it out and read, "Happy anniversary to our greatest treasure. You are our window to heaven, and we want you to know how much we love you. In all the world, there is no treasure better than you!"

As Momma closed the lid on the chest, she had tears in her eyes.

"This is the best gift anyone could have given me because it came from your hearts. I want you to know that this means everything to me. I love you all so much! Thank you for being the best family I could ever ask for."

ABOUT THE AUTHOR

Patrick has always dreamed about writing and telling stories. Franklin the Fearless and His Greatest Treasure began as an idea for a treasure hunt for his wife on their 9th wedding anniversary. It evolved into this story to show his appreciation to his wife for everything she does for their family. This book introduces 2 characters, based on their boys Thomas and Matthew, and the fictional pirate Franklin the Fearless. Franklin will be featured in the author's next book along with his pirate friends. As someone who is physically challenged, it is important to the author to show young people who might feel overwhelmed or burdened by their challenges, that with hard work and a dream…ANYTHING is possible. Every Thomas and Matthew Adventure or Franklin the Fearless story will feature a lesson that encourages hard work and imagination while teaching young people values like friendship and respect.